Published in the United Kingdom in 2016 by Curious Fox
an imprint of Capstone Global Library Limited,
264 Banbury Road, Oxford, OX2 7DY
Registered company number: 6695582
www.curious-fox.com

First published by Stone Arch Books
a Capstone imprint
1710 Roe Crest Drive
North Mankato, MN 56003
www.mycapstone.com

STAR35964

ISBN 978 1 78202 480 4
19 18 17 16 15
10 9 8 7 6 5 4 3 2 1

A full catalogue record for this book is available from the British Library

Contributing artists: Dan Schoening, Erik Doescher, Mike DeCarlo, Lee Loughridge
Designed by Hilary Wacholz

Printed and bound in China

DC COMICS™
SUPER HEROES

AN
ORIGIN STORY

WRITTEN BY
MATTHEW K. MANNING

ILLUSTRATED BY
LUCIANO VECCHIO

Everything is quiet. A spaceship plummets towards Earth. No one can hear the whine of the ship's engines. There is no sound in space.

But inside the craft, things are different. The whir of the computer controls is loud. The emergency alarms are deafening.

This alien is called Abin Sur. He comes from a world far away from our own.

He is a champion on his world. But his time is almost at an end...

"Ring," Abin Sur says. "Find my replacement. Find a man on this world ... a man who knows no fear. Find the next Green Lantern."

The ring's answer can't be heard over the roaring flames. The ship is no longer in outer space. It has entered Earth's atmosphere.

There is nothing quiet about this man or his plane. His name is Hal Jordan. Flying is what he does best.

"You're taking it too high," someone says through Hal's headset. The voice belongs to Carol Ferris, Hal's boss.

He should really listen to her. But he doesn't. Instead, Hal takes the plane higher.

"I'm a test pilot, Carol," Hal says. "I'm going to do my job. Let's see what this thing can do!"

The jet continues to climb. Just then, the engines shut off. "Wait," Hal says. He looks down at his controls. There's no noise coming from them.

Carol's radio goes silent. "Hal?"
Carol yells into her headset. "Hal,
answer me!" But it's silent on the
other end.

Hal pulls at the controls. They don't respond. He only has a few seconds to eject before the plane crashes.

Suddenly, everything starts to glow. A bright, emerald-green light floods the cockpit.

It takes thirty seconds for Hal's eyes to adjust. He can see again. But it takes him much longer to believe his eyes.

His plane is no longer falling. It's flying, lifted up by the strange green light.

The light finally sets the plane down. Hal doesn't recognize the area. There's too much smoke to see anything.

Then a green beam of light cuts through the smoke.

Hal follows the beam through the smoke. The craft on the other end of the light is waiting for him. Its cockpit opens.

Abin Sur speaks. It is in a language Hal has never heard.

The ring on Abin Sur's finger translates for him. "Greetings," the ring says. "You must be the one I'm looking for."

Hal isn't sure what to say. So he says nothing. "You are not … running away at the sight of me," Abin Sur says. "That tells me the ring has chosen correctly. Your bravery and…"

But the alien is too weak to say any more. He simply hands Hal Jordan his ring.

The ring touches Hal's fingers.

Abin Sur disappears. And so does the ship, fire and smoke. All that's left is Hal, the ring and a glowing green lantern.

Hal pauses. Then he slips the ring on his own finger.

Hal takes a step back. Visions fill his mind. Beings in uniforms fly through the sky. They are on some distant world.

Somehow, Hal knows them – even though he has never seen them before.

They are defenders and heroes.

The vision ends. Hal looks down. He sees that he's wearing that same uniform. He has become one of the defenders.

Carol's voice crackles from the jet's radio. "Hal?" she says. "Can you hear me? Are you there?"

"Great," Hal says under his breath. "How am I gonna get this thing airborne again?"

Then a bolt of green bursts from Hal's ring. It surrounds the jet. The jet rises into the air.

"Oh," he says. "That'll work!"

Hal takes a deep breath. He smiles. Then he concentrates and bends his knees. He jumps into the air.

And just keeps on going.

Hal smiles. This is a whole new way of flying. Using his power ring, Hal has created a giant magnet to carry the jet.

Soon Hal is back at the Ferris
Aircraft base. He calmly walks to
the control tower. "Hal!" Carol cries.
"How did you –?"

But the explanation will have
to wait. Another plane has lost
power. It's going down quickly. The
alien radiation from Abin Sur's
damaged ship still hangs in the air.
It is interfering with the plane's
equipment.

With all eyes on the sky, Hal slips out of the room. He touches his ring to his lantern to charge it.

The ring sparks with energy.

Like a bolt of lightning, Hal shoots
into the sky. He grits his teeth. He
aims his ring.

The ring hums. Energy surrounds
the falling plane. Hal closes his eyes.
He concentrates.

Hal gently sets the plane down.

"Wait!" Carol calls after him. "Who are you? How did you do that?!"

For once in his life, Hal Jordan keeps quiet. He just smiles at Carol. Then he turns and flies away.

Hal travels to a distant planet called Oa, home of the Green Lantern Corps. There he will learn the Green Lantern's oath...

"In brightest day, in blackest night, no evil shall escape my sight. Let those who worship evil's might, beware my power ... Green Lantern's light!"

Hal will use his willpower to defeat his foes. He will protect Earth and all the beings of Space Sector 2814 against evil. He is the greatest Green Lantern!

GREEN LANTERN

REAL NAME: HAL JORDAN

ROLE: INTERGALACTIC GUARDIAN

BASE: SPACE SECTOR 2814

A former test pilot, Hal Jordan has learned to remain calm under pressure. But it takes all the willpower he has to be the greatest Green Lantern!

Hal's power ring gives him a variety of amazing powers.

Green Lantern wears a mask to keep his true identity a secret.

Hal's ring shields him from harm.

Using his ring, Hal can create any object he can imagine.

All members of the Green Lantern Corps wear uniforms.

Hal can fly - even in deep space.

The greater a Green Lantern's willpower is, the stronger the objects created by the ring become.

THE AUTHOR

Over the course of MATTHEW K. MANNING's writing career, he has written comics or books starring Batman, Superman, the Flash, the Justice League and even Bugs Bunny. Some of his more recent works include *The Batman Files*, a graphic novel retelling of *The Fall of the House of Usher*, and several DC Super Heroes books. He lives in Connecticut, USA, with his wife Dorothy and daughter Lillian.

THE ILLUSTRATOR

LUCIANO VECCHIO has experience in illustration, animation and comics, and his works have been published in the UK, USA, Spain, France and Argentina. His credits include Ben 10 (DC Comics), Cruel Thing (Norma), Unseen Tribe (Zuda Comics) and Sentinels (Drumfish Productions). He lives in Buenos Aires, Argentina.

GLOSSARY

atmosphere various gases that surround a planet or star

champion someone who fights or speaks publicly in support of something

concentrate think about something or focus on something specific

deafening extremely loud

interfering stopping, slowing or preventing someone or something

plummet fall suddenly straight down (usually from a very high up place)

radiation energy that comes from a source in the form of waves or rays you cannot see. Radiation is often harmful.

recognize know or remember someone or something because of previous knowledge or experience

willpower strong determination that allows you to do something difficult, or the ability to control yourself

DISCUSSION QUESTIONS

Write down your answers. Refer back to the story for help.

QUESTION 1.

Hal flies through the air. We see lines in the background. Why are these lines shown? What do they mean?

QUESTION 2.

Hal uses his ring to create a giant magnet, and then he uses the magnet to carry his aircraft back to base. What are some other ways Hal could have used his power ring to take the plane back?

READ THEM ALL!!

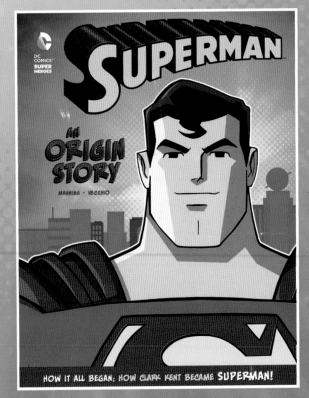

QUESTION 3.

How did Abin Sur find Hal? Why do you think the ring choose Hal to be Abin's replacement?

QUESTION 4.

Where does this line of green energy lead? Who is creating it, and why? How do you know?